fractured

To receive new fiction, contest deadlines,
and other curated content right to
your inbox, send an email to
newsletter@fracturedlit.com

Fractured Lit Volume 2
Stories Selected by Deesha Philyaw
Edited by Tommy Dean

Front cover and interior design
by Cynthia Young and Julianne Johnson

ISBN: 978-1-73636-957-9
Printed in the USA

fractured

volume 2

contents

introduction

One thing that struck me about the twenty surprising and arresting stories I selected for this collection is that none of them are about the pandemic. There are no references to COVID-19 nor to the perils and uncertainties of pandemic life. And yet, the stories are very much of the moment. The characters in these stories are people just trying to hold on—to life or what's left of it, and to those whom they care about.

We're living in both extraordinary and ordinary times right now. Like the characters here, we're all aging, and some of us are caring for our parents as they age. Some of us are remembering who our parents were and what that cost us. Like the characters, we're falling in love, and we're breaking up. We're having babies, and we're losing babies. We're screaming. We're grieving. We are heartbroken. We're dealing with the cruelty of adolescence (and of adolescents). We're fighting for control. Deep down, we crave a reprieve from it all. We want to get back to normal, whatever that is. In one story, *normal* is a troubled couple having sex in The Haunted Mansion at the most magical place on Earth. Nice work if you can get it.

All of the stories here embody the best of what flash can do. With intimate, precise language and voices that are sometimes raw, sometimes tender, these compact stories illuminate deep truths about love and survival. Their themes are both timely and timeless. I don't think it's accurate to say that these stories offer hope. But I can say that in reading them, I felt less alone.

—*Deesha Philyaw*

1

Caterpillar Killer

SHASTRI AKELLA

My friends feared heights and fires. Oceans and flights. I feared insects especially in bar toilets. Until, that is, I met the man at Frisbees.

He grinned when I named myself. Indian names are harder to say than 'Czechoslovakia,' he declared. I am going to call you Boy, he informed me. He necked and humped me on the dance bar's faux leather couch, pressing me down on a mess of hastily put down jackets and purses.

He called it a tasting tour.

He was checking the goods for defects, he said.

He spoke over Cher remixed with the Beatles. His eyes glowed in the dim overhead lights, his wet lips split into a grin.

We danced to the Bee Gees and The Carpenters. It was billed as the 'Queer the Retro' Night. Queers invading the songs of the hippies with their gay hip moves, the reckless grinding of strangers. Why the hell not? Except that Northampton's queer parties are full of straights. The few gay boos that are there come in pairs. The single gay man in a gay bar is a rare species. That's the only reason he picked me, I thought, he certainly wasn't spoiled for choice, this handsome bloke with White Jesus hair and trucker armpits.

After the fifth tequila shot, I went to the bathroom, lumbering down a narrow corridor that was low-lit and smelled of piss.

By the time I was done, my body had a tenant. Once upon a time a caterpillar lived under the commode's rim; now my body was his hiding place.

Back in the corridor that everyone called dirty, some in voices admiring, some in voices that were judgy, I stumbled to the left, skewing a framed photo of the Buddha sitting under a banyan. I collided with two men who were being naughty. English was my third language, so I was especially proud to know those men were called jerkoff buddies.

I took the trucker home and became a dog for him. I even tried to bark, but my throat felt thick, all of its sounds emptied.

He dropped his pants, and the clink of his belt against the wooden floor was a bomb detonating. He placed his big hands on my body and made room for himself, but nothing happened. I feared that he'd wilted.

Wait, what? he said.

He pressed the cold edge of his phone to the small of my back, brought to life its severe white glare, and leaned closer.

What's going on, I asked him.

You got a caterpillar making merry in there, he said, breaking into a gruff, smoker's laughter.

I said, Leave it.

He called me his twisted brownie. He tossed his phone away. He let out a somewhat pained gasp as he slipped in.

Like the wind left his lungs without his will.

Like my body was his wound that felt raw.

Like I was the ugly that tested how far his pity went.

Then he snorted and went to work in earnest. And I cried as I felt the small death wiggle inside me. But I cried quietly. Trucker-Jesus deserved a good time in my humble opinion.

He fucked me as he crushed the caterpillar.

No.

He crushed the caterpillar as he fucked me.

He took the bed, and I took the floor when it was time to sleep. Two butterflies flew out of my mouth, I dreamed. They powdered my dry lips with saffron.

But butterflies aren't born as twins, I thought when I woke up.

The man I could never have was already awake. He slipped one hand then the other into his striped blue shirt as he sat on the edge of the bed.

Don't get funny any ideas, he said as he buttoned up with his back to me.

He told me he had a wife and a six-year-old.

Boy's name's Patrick, he said. A masculine name, he emphasized. Sleep made his voice gruff.

You should do what Asians do, he advised. Change your Indian name to Ken or Walter or something.

Is 'Something' also a name option, I wanted to ask him. But he got up and the moment for the joke had passed.

He said, I'm off, without turning.

You never called me Boy, I said to the empty room. I wanted him to come back, I wanted him to sandpaper me down to nothingness with his blonde stubble.

I went back to Frisbees next Friday looking for my caterpillar killer but failed to find him. So I bought tequila shots for a good-looking lad and his boyfriend and made up stories in my head. The trucker I imagined didn't know I was Bangladeshi.

⌒⌒

SHASTRI AKELLA's debut novel, *The Sea Elephants,* is forthcoming from Flatiron Books (May 2023). He's a 2021-2022 writing fellow at the Fine Arts Works Center in Provincetown, and a 2023 writing fellow of the Oak Springs Garden Foundation fellowship. His writing has appeared or is forthcoming in *Guernica, Fairy Tale Review, Popshot Quarterly, CRAFT, The Masters Review, Electric Literature, Rumpus, PANK, Solstice, The Common,* and *World Literature Review,* among other places.

2

Dirty Shirley

SHANNON BOWRING

They say she'll do anything for a tenner.

She's fourteen. She lives in the trailer park across the river. Sometimes in late spring when the ice goes out, the bridge closes to traffic and the school bus has to stop at the dirt lot of the Fish & Game so she can hop on and hop off. Walk across the bridge alone. Dwayne, the driver, greets her every morning with a smoker's-rasp hello when she climbs the three thick steps onto the bus. Always watches to make sure she gets home safe.

Dwayne and the girl's mother, Shirley, were in the same class in high school. Sophomore year, a few months before Shirley took up with Ned Wilkins and dropped out, Dwayne took her to prom. He wore a powder blue tux. She wore a white dress that shined like fish scales under the green-and-purple party lights in the gym. Blonde hair piled on her head. Bright pink lipstick on her teeth. They danced, drank flat punch. Snuck out behind the one-story clapboard school and drank a quart of Boone's she'd nicked from her old man. They watched the stars, the skinny moon. Muffled music from the gym—Tears for Fears, Duran Duran. Spring peepers singing in the brook behind the Thibodeau farm down the road. It was warm for spring in Northern Maine, but he insisted she wear his jacket anyway, and for days afterward, it smelled like her—wine and vanilla and grass. Dwayne kept returning to his closet. Pressing his face to the scratchy fabric. Inhaling.

Nine, ten years ago, Shirley died in a car wreck out on Route 11. Word around town is she was drunk. Hell, who knows, maybe she did it on purpose. The girl belongs to Ned, or so Shirley always said. The girl and Ned live alone in the trailer. Never, in all the years Dwayne's been driving her to and from school, has Ned come outside to say goodbye or greet her.

One day, Dwayne tells himself, one day he'll park the bus and leave those mouthy little fuckers in their cracked leather seats with their dirty jokes, their cruel laughter. He'll leave them behind and take Shirley's daughter's hand and march her to the screen door of the trailer. Pound on the rust-splotched metal until Ned stumbles out and opens it. Tell that selfish asshole what a gift the girl is, warn him about what happens to girls whose fathers don't pay close enough attention.

Anything for a tenner.

They said the same thing about her mother, all those years ago.

She looks so much like Shirley used to. Curly blonde hair, bony wrists, crooked front teeth. Sometimes, something about the way the girl pulls herself up the steps and into the diesel-scented bus reminds Dwayne of his own mother. Of himself. That slow, forward slog. Feet heavy. Eyes down.

SHANNON BOWRING'S work has appeared in numerous journals, has been nominated for a Pushcart and a Best of the Net, and was selected for Best Small Fictions 2021. Her debut novel, *The Road to Dalton*, will be published by Europa Editions in June 2023. Shannon lives in Bath, Maine.

3

Picking Up Stones

WILLIAM BRADLEY

Two-lane rural route to the boatyard, boondock enough for hoedowns, cross-burnings, not that I knew much about either, except they happened, that's all. Downtown Philly boy a little young for my age, I once asked the burly guy who ran the place (clean-shaven, blue checkered shirt, gas company cap) why everyone in sight was white, where was everyone else? And he answered with a slowly widening grin, maybe that's the only kind we want around here.

My dad, so young and wild, driving us to the pea-green river where his Chinese junk was moored, bought for reasons undisclosed. Yet it made him famous for a day in the city paper, a photo of him hunched over sea charts, marking his turtle progress. At each harbor southward people approached, stoked him with questions about his alien craft—blood red sails held taut by bamboo rigging and coiled, scaly dragons carved in teak on the bow, and a stern so canted and high it felt crazy to jump off. But we did.

My sister and I staring through pollen-smudged windows at dense, blurred cornfields. I devoured the newspaper in the back seat—my job to scout the seriously weird or bad stuff and read aloud. A shredded year: in his own driveway, Medgar Evers shot, killed, police guardian mysteriously absent. Dad said, "Don't worry, Kennedy will get to the bottom of this." Bomb crater in the ladies' lounge, Birmingham church. JFK's casket hauled down Pennsylvania Avenue, a riderless black horse tossing its head, pawing the ground, empty boots reversed in the stirrups. Dad insisting, "Things have to get better, believe me."

Glanced up to see a white rectangle with plain black letters, a town's name flicking by—a disaster looping back to me. I recounted all the details to my sister and dad, though they kept saying, "That's enough—you can stop now." *The* Clipper Tradewind *circled these fields during a thunderstorm, waiting for the signal to land. Five people on the ground saw a ball of fire after lightning hit. The black box saved the pilot's last words: "Here we go." Six thousand bits of debris: twisted metal, melted plastic, bone splinters, scraps of flesh. All that stuff packed in crates and hauled to a giant metal shed. They wanted to put it back together like a puzzle.* Then I stopped, resumed staring out the window. By my rules, these fields should have looked different than they did, stay scarred, left unsown. Yet they were fully planted, luxuriant, managing only a vegetable peace.

Out of gas, the car coasted to a stop on a slight rise, framed by cornstalks on each side of the road. Dad would let this kind of thing happen. Take us to a drugstore, tell us we could stock up on comic books from the rotating metal rack—then sweet-talk the sourpuss cashier, who was right to doubt his check was any good. Dad said we were close to help but couldn't say how close. He switched to a deep funny roaring voice, a little hoarse, just right for a tale of a bloated king or monster: *OK, kiddies, let's lace up our hiking boots, time for an adventure!* No hiking boots; just sneakers. I pushed the door open, heavy, a vault.

I was a little young for my age; needed everything explained, spelled out. Clean-shaven face of the boatyard guy, his blue checkered shirt, his slowly widening grin... *the only kind we want around here.*

The way we walked was uphill, the same direction we'd been going. No traffic—but you couldn't see what might be rushing over that asphalt rise—just the crinkling waves of heat bracketing the road. Shifting to another strange voice, taut and severe, Dad ordered us to pick up stones on the shoulder, keep a few big ones in each hand. He was scared of rabid creatures that roamed this kind of country; told us that more than once. Walking up the road, I returned to the plane that circled above the fields, aiming to skirt hard weather, hoping the squall line would creep to another map. I found three mud-caked stones and gripped them tight.

Notes: Medgar Evers, civil rights activist, was assassinated on June 12, 1963, in Jackson, Mississippi. The bombing of the 16th Street Baptist Church in Birmingham, Alabama, occurred on September 15, 1963, resulting in the deaths of four children. The Clipper Tradewind, a commercial airliner, crashed near Elkton, Maryland, December 1963, killing all eighty-one on board.

Writing by WILLIAM BRADLEY has appeared in such journals as *Carolina Quarterly, Cimarron Review, Denver Quarterly, Nashville Review, Post Road,* and *Willow Springs.*

4

Giving Up

CATHY CADE

My sister turns her key in the lock and pushes. The door moves a handbreadth.

Mum croaks from the living room. "Hang on—I'm coming."

She grunts as she bends to move the draught excluder guarding the door, and we are assailed by the familiar onslaught of lavender air freshener.

In the kitchen, we unpack the shopping we've brought her, and Pam goes to open the cupboard under the sink.

"Not there—I've had a shift around." Mum coughs. "Leave the laundry tablets. I'll put 'em away later. You make us a cuppa."

Pam abandons the laundry tablets on the worktop and dips into the shopping bag again. "I don't like the sound of that cough," she scolds.

I fill the kettle.

The floral caddy behind the kettle is empty of tea bags so I refill it from the box in the cupboard over the sink. As I return the pack, I spot the engraved cigarette lighter Dad gave Mum on their silver wedding anniversary, tucked between the sugar and the stock cubes. Maybe she's afraid Pam will tell her to throw it away.

We almost lost Mum to bronchitis last winter. Her breathing was so bad she couldn't smoke for weeks. Pam insisted it was time Mum gave it up as she would already be over the nicotine withdrawal period. Weakened by illness and fed up with Pam's nagging, she'd yielded.

Not that Pam knows what withdrawal is like. Neither of us got into the smoking habit. Mum and Dad had both smoked since their teens; tobacco carried Mum through wartime fire-watching in East London. Even after Dad's death from lung cancer in his sixties, Mum's previous attempts to give it up failed. Miserably.

Pam takes a twin-pack of tissues into the abandoned dining room where Mum stores spare packs of stuff. She reappears brandishing a 200-pack of duty-free cigarettes. "What's this, then?"

"Oh… Stuart stopped by on his way home from the airport. He never remembers I've given up." Our brother lives up north. We don't see much of him.

Pam fumes. "Is he trying to kill you off?"

"Probably." Mum is always disappointed that his visits are so brief. "Maybe he's in a hurry for his share of my house when I'm gone."

She always makes the spare room ready in case he stays over, but he never does.

"Well, I'm throwing these away," declares Pam.

Mum rallies. "No, leave them in there. I'm giving them to Jean."
I've never seen her neighbour with a cigarette, but I say nothing and Pam stomps back to the front room, tutting.

While the kettle boils, I make space for shoeshine among a drawer stuffed with old polish tins and a can of lighter fuel. The mugs on the draining board would benefit from a rinse; Mum doesn't always wear her glasses when she's washing up.

In the sink, a filter-tipped dog-end is wedged in the drain filter. I push it through and turn on the tap.

CATHY CADE is a retired librarian. Her writing has been published in *Scribble, Best of British, Tales of the Forest, Sirens Call, Writers Forum, Seven Days, The Fens, Flash Fiction Magazine,* and anthologies like *The Poet* and the To Hull and Back short story competition. Cathy lives with her husband and dogs—most of the time in Cambridgeshire surrounded by flat Fenland fields. The rest of the time she lives across the fence from London's Epping Forest. Her published stories are available from Amazon and Smashwords. Find Cathy at www.cathy-cade.com.

5

In the Closet

GRACE ELLIOTT

When you start needing a place to scream, you try most of the rooms in the house.

You start with the shower. At first, you take a weird pleasure in screaming behind the shower curtain. In college, you had a film major roommate, and the two of you would take over the dorm lounge on Saturday nights. While everyone else got their kicks with underage drinking, you two would watch old films. *Psycho* was the roommate's favorite.

But *Psycho* has created its scars. Or perhaps too many accidents happen in the bathroom for it to be a good place to scream. One small howl—not even enough to make your throat ache—brings your son rushing in.

"Mommy? Mommy?" he says.

At least he cares, you think as you pull the shower curtain around yourself and stick your head out to assure him you're not hurt.

"There's a bake sale at school today," he says. "Did you make cookies?"

"What bake sale?" you ask.

THAT NIGHT, YOU try screaming into your pillow. You've heard a lot about that, it's downright clichéd. A marriage counselor even recommended it to you, once. One of the early ones your husband liked.

You scream for a minute, and for some reason you think about a production of *Othello* you were in in high school. The girl playing Desdemona was a friend of yours, a shy girl who was reluctant to be on stage at all, but who gave that final scene everything she had.

You scream and try to recall the story at the same time—was Desdemona cheating? Or was that Othello? You know this much, Desdemona did not press the pillow to her own face as you are doing. In the middle of a satisfying scream, your husband's snores stop abruptly. He asks if you could please go to sleep.

The pillow is now moist from your tongue and teeth and desperate, spitting breath. You turn it over and wonder what else will go in the laundry with the pillowcase in the morning.

YOU THINK YOU'VE really found it, the perfect place to scream: in the closed garage, inside the locked car, with the motor running to drown out the noise. But then your husband comes down to get his car out. He's going to pick up the oldest child for soccer.

"Don't pull a Sylvia Plath," he jokes when he sees you there, red faced from the screaming but suddenly silent in his company.

"A Sylvia Plath?"

"She killed herself with gas, didn't she?"

Afterward, you will look this up and discover that Plath killed herself in an oven, not a minivan. Your husband had his symbols of femininity/available suicide methods mixed up. You consider telling him this, but the thought of his distracted replies makes you want to scream some more. Besides, you have to pick up the younger children for swimming. You don't have time.

YOU WONDER IF the closet with the spare bedding would make a good screaming spot. You've always liked the way it smelled—like your brand-new house and the mixture of your husband's cologne and your own perfume. And you think that the space might be cozy, in there with all those blankets. But, ultimately, you don't give it a try. You have been avoiding that closet for weeks now, since finding the condoms you did not buy, the fluorescent lingerie you would have mocked if you had seen it in the store. You screamed when you found all that, and the oldest of your children ran to you at once. She is a sweet girl, a good girl, just entering puberty, just starting to agree to watch your rom-coms with you on weekday nights when her father is working late.

"What?" she said, there in that closet. And you hurried to hide what you had found, even though you couldn't stop screaming. Soon, you gathered a crowd. One frightened child you had to lie to and put back in bed, one just old enough to be wary at your insistence that there was a spider, one who will almost certainly remember this later and blame you, as you now blame your mother, for failing to leave a man who deserves to be left.

No. Clearly, that closet won't work for private screaming again.

INSTEAD YOU WALK around your house—your perfect house—and remember when you used to scream outdoors, in the open. When your screams were to encourage the Red Sox or shoo a raccoon, when you were not afraid of what would come out if you opened your mouth in public. Those screams, as you recall them, were satisfying, but they weren't necessary. If the Red Sox ignored your hollering, then they would not miss the school bus or forget their homework or skip out into the street and get hit by a car. And that raccoon? It could have your trash. It's your marriage you now want to protect from the woman leaving behind her trashy laundry, the husband tipping over the metaphorical recycling bins of your life and threatening to scatter your secrets in the street.

AND SO, YOU find your places to scream. The garage, like Plath, as you now think of it; the pillow, like Desdemona; and the shower, like that woman from *Psycho* whose name you can't remember. Slowly, day by day, you become hoarse.

"What's wrong, babe?" your husband asks when you finally lose your voice entirely.

You look at him, but you cannot reply.

And so, your life, as you know it, does not end. Your husband drives to get the children from soccer, and you bake cookies for bake sales. He snores in bed beside you, and one day, someday, you open the closet with the spare bedding and smell again the mixture of your new house and his cologne and your perfume. And then you close the closet door and go on with your life.

GRACE ELLIOTT is a writer and editor living just outside New York. Her writing has appeared in *Joyland, Electric Literature,* and *Vol. 1 Brooklyn.* She has attended the One Story Writers Conference, Aspen Summer Words, and Tin House's Winter Novel Workshop.

6

Ways of Karst

JAMIE ETHERIDGE

The hole drinks the grass, the leaves, the twigs, and our favorite park bench. Insatiable. Thirsting. It then drinks the sidewalk where little kids and their mothers play games like 'avoid the shark' and 'alphabet hop.' But children don't play on the sidewalks anymore.

You jump right into the middle of the group, your gloves and hat tossed to the ground, and the children gather around you, fluvial and seamless as a conga line. A waterfall of stubby, sneakered feet and flailing hands as the collective wades down the pastel-etched course, hopscotching to a rhyme.

1-2-3-4.
Mama said be home by four.
5-6-7-8.
Mama said don't be late.

⟵

In the beginning no one knows what caused the holes. No one knew what was happening nor why. But I know.

Sinkholes are proof of movement, underground streams etching away limestone, fluting through rock. They coalesce: one depression joining another to create flat floor basins, underground caverns, dissolute rock formations. Known as karst, they are absences, evidence of what was once solid and certain but is now empty, disappeared.

⟵

We play in the park. You on the swings. Me on the bench, watching. Or we buy hot dogs and have a picnic. You climb the dogwoods or throw pennies into the fountain.

"Listen, Mama, I wish..."

"Don't tell me, kiddo, otherwise it won't come true."

You place one finger against pink lips, nod, then close your eyes. I take another sip.

Later we skip across the grass, swinging hands and then hop down the chalked outline, calling out the letters and numbers as we go. You want one more slide, one more turn on the merry-go-round.

So I leave you there, go for a quick nip around the corner.

⟵

Over time the holes multiply. People suggest fencing them in, since they can't be filled, as if anyone can stop a hole, as if a hole can be contained.

Over time the holes grow louder. They echo and judder. Reverberate. They whisper to me, enticing and lucid, like the moment that first drink hits your veins. I hear them calling still, like the wind, sere and desolate, cutting between the skyscrapers, slicing down the sidewalks.

⟵

That's where they found you, crying on the sidewalk, scared and alone.

⟵

Sinkholes devour but also create—space and openings. And I think, maybe the holes aren't holes at all but tunnels connecting me to you. A wormhole to a distant galaxy where mothers and children never separate. Where time and liquid do not matter. Where mistakes can be undone.

This morning I leave the apartment, take the stairs down to street level and buy hot coffee from a street vendor at the corner of the park. My throat aches. But coffee is all I will drink today.

The hole in Washington Square shudders and shimmers when I come near. The liquid black at the center eddies and shakes. I stand at the edge, lean over, look down, wonder if there's any difference between jumping and falling.

⟿

JAMIE ETHERIDGE is creative nonfiction editorial assistant for *CRAFT Literary* and was a finalist for the *Kenyon Review* Developmental Edit 2021 Contest in creative nonfiction. Jamie's writing can be found in *Anti-Heroin Chic, Bending Genres, Essay Daily, Identity Theory, JMWW Journal, Reckon Review, X-R-A-Y Lit* and other publications. Read her work at LeScribbler.com.

7

Sea Bugs

AMANDA HADLOCK

A shrimp's heart is in its head. You used to say your heart was in your stomach when you couldn't get out of bed all day. You won't eat shrimp because your dead dad who you hated used them as bait when he took you catfishing as a kid. I found that out when I made scampi on our six-month anniversary, and you refused to eat it. That made me cry, then me crying made you cry, then we spent the whole night sulking and chain smoking on your back steps instead of eating shrimp and having sex like I had planned.

The commercial shrimping industry rakes in over 50 billion dollars annually. I used to buy the pre-cooked frozen jumbo prawns from Wal-Mart, $4.99 for a pound. That was fancy for a waitress in West Plains. I've never eaten them fresh. I've never been to the coast, any coast. Farthest I've been is Alton, Illinois to visit my grandfather's grave. You wouldn't go with me, either. You said the drive was too long and you don't like my taste in music.

All shrimp are born male. Later in life, their gonads can develop into ovaries. A female shrimp can lay up to 14,000 eggs at once. You knew I'd never wanted children, in fact, we had laughed about our shared distaste toward kids on our first date. We drank a whole bottle of convenience store champagne and had sex for the first time on your kitchen linoleum. In the morning, you fried bacon for breakfast, and we ate the whole pound of it in silence, licked the grease from our fingertips. You told me to come back that night, and I said, *Deal,* and the rest happened fast and slow at the same time.

From conception to death, a shrimp will evolve through 16 different life stages. Depending on who you ask, humans go through 5 to 12. Does this make the shrimp more complex than us? Maybe, I think. I feel like I've gone through 0 life stages sometimes. And sometimes I miss eating those pre-cooked Wal-Mart shrimp, even though I always thought they kind of looked like weird alien embryos. Another thing I gave up for you, even though you never asked me to.

But then again, shrimp skitter around in exoskeletons, they're invertebrates, just like the crickets or cockroaches we crush underfoot in your kitchen sometimes. This makes them sea bugs, technically, fish food. Maybe you're right that they're better suited as bait. Maybe I should pay more attention to what I put into my body.

A shrimp's color is determined by its environment, and the Mantis shrimp can see colors we can't. In the second year, we painted your spare bedroom baby blue for our son-to-be, like a good, God-fearing hetero couple should, laughing together when I joked about that. You were so excited, you said, you would have a family again. We stenciled the name we had chosen for him on the wall in pencil, but I bled him out before we got the chance to color it in. We never did paint over the stencil or erase it. You stayed in bed most days, called in sick. I had lost my appetite. All I could stomach for weeks was stale bread I'd steal bites of at work. I started picking up more double shifts so I wouldn't have to be at home.

Some shrimp can snap their claws loud enough to kill nearby fish or rupture a human eardrum. I put on a hard exterior after we lost our son, thrashed my claws when you tried to come close. We stopped touching each other, stopped talking, stopped sharing meals. I wondered if you found me attractive anymore; you hardly looked at me. I spent hours staring in the bathroom mirror and pinching the folds of fat beneath my arms, between my thighs, across my lower stomach. I imagined taking a pair of kitchen shears and slicing off long, soft strips from my belly, tossing them outside for the turkey vultures. You bought a blow-up mattress and put it in the new spare room, with its walls still painted American Spirit blue and the boy's name stenciled in. You started staying there, away from me, though I can't remember how long it's been. And I sleep better alone now, honestly.

Shrimp can't swim, not really. They can't control their bodies. It's more like an illusion: they propel themselves through the water with small swimmerets they keep concealed beneath their abdomen. They typically move backwards when encountering predators. We've been moving backwards since our son left, eating less, fighting more. *I still love you,* I told you after I snapped at you again the other night. But you couldn't hear me, or you couldn't bring yourself to answer. I can hear you refill your air mattress through the walls sometimes, the motorized air pump growling like a dying animal. I hear you settle in when you try to sleep, the rush of air when you fall into bed, and I can hear you think throughout the night. I wonder if maybe we should repaint the walls. A deeper blue might be nice. Or one of the colors shrimp see that we can't, a shade unimaginable to our small, human minds.

AMANDA HADLOCK is an MFA candidate at Florida State University, where she serves as Assistant Editor of *Southeast Review*. Her work has appeared or is forthcoming in journals such as *Cleaver Magazine, Wigleaf,* NPR/WFSU's *All Things Considered, Essay Daily, The Florida Review,* and others. She is originally from Missouri.

8

Endless Spoonful

SUSIE HARA

We're having lunch at the faux restaurant. My mom is eating her fish at a glacial pace, and I've moved on to dessert. Without warning, she reaches over, scoops up a forkful of my ice cream, and spreads it over her fish. *Disgusting*, I think, but I say nothing. Why? Because we live in Dementia Landia. In this world, it's fine to eat fish with ice cream sauce. In fact, pretty much anything is okay in this ecosphere, as long as you're not hurting anyone.

A young man with expertly twisted hair and a name tag that reads "Faithful" comes to the table to clear the plates. He solemnly examines my mother's dish. "Fish. With ice cream," he states. "I'll have to try that sometime." He says this without irony.

I let out the breath I've been holding and smile at him, a nonverbal thank you for his kindness. It's reassuring that Faithful also abides by the local customs here at the memory care village where he works and my mother lives. He nods gravely and moves on to another table and another story.

We continue with our silent meal. In the world where we used to live, before we were sent to this land, we were writers. Language was our medium, talk our currency. Analyzing, commenting, arguing, gossiping, revealing, bantering, chatting, discussing, joking, bickering, schmoozing, observing, remarking, pronouncing, articulating, proposing, kibitzing, challenging, agreeing, deliberating, and confiding. We talked about the terrors and pleasures of love and marriage. About the many kinds of heartache and loss. About books, plays, movies, friendship, war, peace, poetry, capitalism, communism, injustice, and stupidity. About food, history, sex, and comedy. These days, we still talk, but in much shorter sentences. If I string too many words together, she looks distressed. Sometimes, I lean over and speak directly into her hearing aid. Other times, she'll say, "Slow down."

I'm wolfing down the ice cream when I remember that we had ordered the bowl to share. I put my spoon down. But now, without the sweet dish to sedate me, sadness seeps into the gap. It spreads everywhere. I sigh, blowing out a noisy gust of air. My mom, fastening her empathetic coal black eyes on me, reaches over to stroke my hand. In spite of everything, she's retained her supersonic mother skills. A wave of love sweeps over me, and I curl my hand into hers.

I try to stay in the present, I do, but I'm already racing into the future. Fast-forwarding to this evening. When I will steel myself to leave. When I will say goodbye and she will try to come with me, and I will explain I have to fly back home to San Francisco, and she will insist angrily that she will get on the plane with me, and I will nod in understanding and hug and kiss her goodbye. When I will rush through the lobby, tears pooling, with an almost giddy sigh of relief. When the loudest of the competing voices in my head will rise above the others to accuse: *You are a bad daughter.*

In Dementia Landia, we caregivers tend to have an ongoing soundtrack. A guilt track. We each have a signature version, and mine has a distinctly Jewish rhythm, a sort of davening quality. It goes like this: If only we had enough money for 24-hour caregivers she could be back home, where it would be familiar and comforting. And then she would be happy. If only I had a big house and she could come live with us, and if only that wouldn't make us all insane. If only I had moved her up to be near me in San Francisco. If only I knew the right thing to do.

A childhood image of my mother rises up out of nowhere. She's in the tiny room off the kitchen we called her office, her fingers flying over the typewriter keys, her cigarette burning in the ashtray, writing for hours, far away, in a world of her own making. Late in the afternoon, she stops working just in time to cook dinner for me and my sister and our dad. Maybe she's still there, in a parallel universe, banging on the keys, lost in thought.

My mother is done with her fish combo. She pushes away her plate, and I nudge the bowl of ice cream over to her. She takes a bite, says, "It doesn't taste like anything." Then she takes another spoonful.

I nod and smile, my head bobbing up and down like one of those dolls on the dashboard of a car. How I wish it tasted good to her, and how I wish I could change things. My next bite has a metallic edge. I put the spoon down. I'm so tired. I don't *like* Dementia Landia. I'm lost here. There's no GPS, not even an old-fashioned map. It's not only that I don't know where we are, I don't know when we are. In this land, time is elastic.

My mom tunes into my wavelength again. This time her piercing eyes say *come back*. I make a soft landing, arriving back from hyperspace with a thump.

She points to the ice cream. "Have some more."

I take a bite, and now the metallic edge is gone. It has the round, buttery taste of vanilla beans.

She nods and takes another bite.

We eat slowly.

Together, we finish every last endless spoonful.

SUSIE HARA'S first novel, *Finder of Lost Objects*, was a finalist for a Lambda Literary Award and recipient of an International Latino Book Award. She has worked in theater as a performer, director, and writer. Her stories appear in several anthologies, including *Fast Girls* and *Stirring up a Storm*. Her upcoming novel, *The House on Ashbury Street*, will be published in March 2023. She lives and writes in San Francisco.

9

"Charlotte Sometimes"

ELIOT LI

I'm driving around the Tenderloin on Monday night. Past the homeless encampment, the liquor stores, the iron bars across the doors and windows. The girls in heels and hiked up skirts. It's been a year since my wife Emily died, and I'm not handling it well.

There's a petite girl in a black dress standing at the corner of Leavenworth and O'Farrell. I pull my car over, and she leans against my open window, curly mop of golden hair falling over her eyes. She's shivering in the night air. I open the passenger door, and she gets in.

"Are you a cop?" she asks, reaching over to pinch me between my legs.

"I'm not a cop. Are you?"

"No. You can touch my breast." She cups my palm to the front of her dress. Her fingers are icy, but her chest feels warm.

I say what I want to do, and she tells me how much it'll cost. The girl's voice is soft, low and even. Emily's voice.

I drive her to the Trocadero in the warehouse district, the red brick building near the shipyards. Monday nights are "The Death Guild," the weekly goth dance club. People in black line up at the entrance.

Once inside, we walk across the dark space, through a twisting crowd of dancers, some gaunt and bony, others buxom and voluptuous, all squeezed into leather and fishnets, or silk Victorian dresses, with black lipstick and heavy eye shadow, spiked hair dyed purple, red, and green. The smell of sweaty leather and cannabis.

I think I see Emily in the corner dancing by herself, though it's not really her. A woman gyrating in a latex body suit, laces pulled tight across her cleavage. Emily liked to come here in her full vinyl body suits. Her favorite was bright turquoise, and when she wore it, shiny and iridescent, she was a light against all that darkness on the dance floor. The zipper was in the back, where she couldn't reach, so I'd zip it up for her, stretching the glossy material over her hips and shoulders. Healthy Emily, before the chemo.

The girl I'm paying, she tries hard to please, moving to the music, with small steps and jerky arm motions, and her polite smile. This likely isn't where she would choose to hang out.

The Cure's "Charlotte Sometimes" echoes through the dance hall, Robert Smith's voice ghost-like and gloriously out of tune.

FIFTEEN YEARS AGO, Emily and I cut our college classes, and took the bus to misty Half Moon Bay.

On the beach, we watched the elephant seals lounging on the rocks. "The alpha male," she whispered, pointing to a bloated gray mass with an enormous proboscis, surrounded by smaller females. "Harems are so disgusting."

She turned to face the ocean. Holding her arms out, she started singing "Killing an Arab."

"Do you know what novel inspired Robert Smith to write that song?" I asked.

"Of course," she said. "Camus' *L'Etranger!*"

She took off and ran into the waves, the hem of her skirt wet with ocean water.

My heart overflowed. A woman who was obsessed with monogamy and literature. And The Cure.

THE GIRL I'M paying is with me in the men's bathroom, down in the basement. The beat of the music thumps through the ceiling. The toilet seat is cracked, splashed with urine. The lights flicker.

I press her against the side of the stall, my hands under her dress. The girls I pay usually don't kiss, but when our lips touch, her tongue shoots past my teeth, searching inside my mouth. She undoes my pants. The belt buckle clinks against the hard, sticky floor.

Emily and I did it here once, and then never again. Outside of our bedroom, she wanted it to be somewhere beautiful, somewhere sacred. Stow Lake under the moonlight, blanket spread out on the grassy banks.

Sex in the Trocadero's shitty bathroom was debasing, she said.

I PULL THE car to the curb on Leavenworth and unfold the bills from my wallet. This young woman's given me "the girlfriend experience." It's supposed to be rare, and I pay her more than what we'd settled on. She steps outside. She's already looking into the windows of other cars.

I put The Cure's *Faith* CD into the car stereo and turn the volume up as I drive away.

I think I hear Emily's voice in the car. She's singing along with the music. It's late, and we're heading home together after another Monday night at The Death Guild.

"Honey, I've debased myself again," I say, turning to her. "I can't stop."

Emily's lipstick is smudged. It runs across the side of her face, but she smiles, her cheeks plump and flushed.

She just keeps singing.

ELIOT LI lives in California. His work appears or is forthcoming in *SmokeLong Quarterly, Pithead Chapel, Lunch Ticket, Juked, The Pinch, Cleaver, Flash Frog,* and others.

10

The Magic Kingdom

ELIOT LI

"I still think we can make this work," I say, as we approach Walt and Mickey on their floral cement pedestal, in the middle of the theme park.

She won't even look at me.

Bronze Walt reaches his arm out to bestow happiness upon us. I almost trip on the cobblestones along Main Street, U.S.A. The Walk of Magical Memories. One of these faded red octagon pavers has our names engraved on it. *Mingxia loves William, XOXO.* We can't seem to find our brick anymore.

She maintains her silence, while we walk under the arches of Sleeping Beauty's castle. Three years ago, we had said our vows in front of this castle, her bridal gown aglow in purple fairy tale light.

Tonight, another fight in our living room. She threw the first punch. Said I provoked her by calling her overbearing mother a pig. I said back when we got married, she promised that her mother would stay in Taiwan, not two doors down.

Mingxia has a powerful right hook.

We slumped to the floor together, exhausted and depressed. We said it's finally over. Then, somehow, I convinced her to come with me to the Magic Kingdom again.

"The Haunted Mansion," I say, as we pass the funnel cake stand. "Do you want to go?"

A partially formed smile breaks through the sadness on her face. She's thinking about it now, what we once did inside that mansion with the wrought iron railings and marble columns. We head to New Orleans Square, our steps quickening, as we detour past Thunder Mountain.

OUR DOOM BUGGY cogwheels around, revealing the tilting candelabra in the infinity hallway, the row of self-knocking doors, Madame Leota's '80s metal band hair floating in a glass sphere. The organ music, the whistling wind. I search with my fingertips for the back of her hand. She might pull away if I actually touch her. The lightning through the fake window. It lights up the inside of our buggy. She's not looking at Madame Leota. Her eyes are on me.

The beating heart bride, red light flickering underneath her bosom. The low thumping sound in the darkness. Mingxia knows it gets me excited every time. She pulls my head to her chest so I can hear her heartbeat.

We descend the hill, and the graveyard ghost party comes into view.

"Let's do it," she says. I grin like the hatbox ghost.

We squeeze under the safety bar and hop out in front of the opera singing busts, laughing while we take our places behind the tombstones. We crouch down, then take turns jumping up quick, arms out like scarecrows, shrieking, before slowly sliding back down.

"*Asian* ghouls," an older lady says. "That's new."

"Animatronics getting more realistic every year," her companion says.

When we tire of scaring people, we join the trio of hitchhiking ghosts at the end of the ride, holding our thumbs out toward the exit, showcasing our biggest fake smiles. The confused look of the riders, the children poking their parents and saying, "Those aren't real ghosts." We retreat into the darkness.

I RUB THE bruise on my shoulder. Scrape the tender scab from where she drew blood on the side of my face. It still stings. The rusty metallic scent of blood on my fingertips.

"Let's go entertain the Mummy," she says.

"I'm not sure."

The Mummy, wrapped in white bandages, sits on his sarcophagus, glass of tea in hand, tipping his head back in laughter.

Mingxia pushes me down, behind gravestones in the shadows. She tosses my clothes at the plastic tree. The ghosts popping and squealing, the wolves howling, my wife thrusting on top of me, my tears mixing with blood on my cheek, and the Mummy just stares at us and laughs.

ELIOT LI lives in California. His work appears or is forthcoming in *SmokeLong Quarterly, Pithead Chapel, Lunch Ticket, Juked, The Pinch, Cleaver, Flash Frog,* and others.

11

Flossing

ANITA LO

Mom flosses me every night with my limbs starfished across the kitchen counter and my head hanging off the edge. She kneels over me with a spool of minted thread and works the string between my teeth. She says nothing used to come out of there, just berry skins and basil, and I would pop my mouth closed like a little coin purse. Nowadays, cheap rhinestones and cigarettes leap from my gums, and she wipes her hands on an old blue bath towel that's growing green. Then she sends me to my room where I dream of having a cartoon smile, unbroken upper and lower strips of white for teeth.

For lunch Mom packs me sliced fruit soaked in saltwater so that it doesn't brown, so that even when cut open for hours it looks fresh. It is just as pristine when I bring it home uneaten. Other kids buy lunch from the cafeteria: cheeseburgers frilled with greens, red-drowned spaghetti, juicy slices of pizza. Julia says it's gross, but I eat her crusts at the end of lunch hour, covering my face in leftover salt and oil. Those nights, the floss gets so greasy and orange that it barely stays wound around Mom's fingers. She knots it around her thumbs so that it doesn't slip away, and by the end the tips are purpled like sausages, which makes me so embarrassed for her, losing her grip and killing herself over it.

Julia and I collect little trophies from the classrooms: protractors and staplers and the history teacher's glasses and the art teacher's aprons. She hides them in her dad's car and I pocket them in my mouth. Julia gives me the principal's mousepad that Mom flosses from between my canines; I grab for it as she tries to toss it over her shoulder. I am almost as tall as her now, but what scares her back is my blood-lined gums.

Mom always says we need to be extra careful because girls in our family are born with only one set of teeth. That others have the option of a fresh start when their adult teeth push the baby teeth out of their cradles, but our family sold that right in order to board a ship and come here. "If girls here don't like what they have, they pull out the tooth and start over," she whispers to me while she flosses, a staple flecking her cheek. "But we only have one chance."

That's also why she won't show me her teeth. "We had no floss when I was young," she says. "They're full of junk." She covers her mouth with both hands when she laughs or smiles or shouts. Every time she tells the boat story, our family is at sea for longer and longer, and by now we're adrift for years between basement apartments and restaurant attics before Mom says, "Finally, I had you." I imagine Mom at the stern of a ship trying to work a bottle cap from between her molars with her tongue, fingers tight on the gunwale, ocean spray brining her lips.

"Do I floss?" says Julia, draining a can of Coca-Cola in one breath. "I mean, when the dentist makes me." She crushes the can and hiss-laughs when the aluminum cuts her. I lick the blood off her palm, and it's thick, rich, the flavor of someone brave. I study the veins in the pale of our wrists and suspect that they look the same.

On weekends Mom hard-boils eggs or heats a bowl of fish congee for us to share. I can hardly sit through our sterile breakfast before running down the street to 7-Eleven where Julia is waiting in the car, M&M bags wedged between seat cushion, the school gym's Exit sign lopsided in the rear window. This week she shows me how to slip bracelets into my bra at Claire's and how to dine-and-dash, and my mouth grows heavy with jewels.

Mom buys extra boxes of floss now, bulk packs that should last years but that we go through in days, because she lashes me to the passenger seat when she picks me up after school, so I don't run away, so that she can wiggle matchsticks of salted pear between my lips and floss me again before bed. My teeth snap at her fingers, but I swear I am just trying to ask a question.

Over spring break, Julia and I are running from the mall cops, and I trip over a seam in the asphalt, knocking out my top right incisor. Mom finds me in the kitchen holding a towel-wrapped ice pack to my mouth. "Let me see," she says, and moans when I show her the gap, and then the forlorn bloody pebble in my hand. She puts the lost tooth in milk and binds me to the kitchen counter.

That night, gently exploring the jellied wound with my tongue, I discover a needle of enamel poking through my gum. I wriggle free of the floss and wake Mom, whose cheeks are still lacquered with tears.

"New tooth," I say, something golden ballooning in my chest. She presses her lips tighter and peers inside, but even she can't miss the whitish nub barely crowning.

"It's not possible," she says, her eyes unfocused.

"You were lying, you're always lying to me," I scream. "I'm not like you!" She crumples to the counter and lets me run to my room unclean.

I wake up later that night to a light in the kitchen. Gums itching, head pounding, I discover Mom kneeling on the linoleum, a tangle of floss in her hands. "Come here," she says, and this time she lies down, arms and legs spanning the counter as if she's floating in water. She drops her jaw and tilts her head back, and I gasp at all the colors.

ANITA LO lives in New York City. Her work has appeared or is forthcoming in the *Vestal Review, Fractured Lit,* and AAWW's *The Margins.*

12

Arcade Neophytes

SARAH MATSUI

Mom and I got really into the arcade claw machine one elementary school summer.

Handful of tokens, a frappé from the neighboring cafe, ready. We aren't even coffee drinkers.

Our eyes scan a sea of tightly packed yellow polyester lions with auburn manes.

"哪個?"

"That one."

We speak different first languages, but I understand her question, and she can see which plush toy I'm pointing at.

This linguistic margin is bridgeable; it's nothing compared to our contradicting visions for how daughters, mothers, ought to be: "你怎麼變成那麼黑? 頭髮亂七八糟. 胖死掉." *How did you get to be so dark? Your hair is such a mess. So fat we could die.*

No one else but her cares when I play in the sun or let my hair get wild. No one else calls me fat.

"這是你爸的錯." *This is your dad's fault.*

She was the one who chose to marry him.

"如果你是別人的女兒,我不管." *If you were someone else's daughter, I wouldn't care.*

I had in fact, at various points, wished I were someone else's daughter.

"我應該回台灣." *I should go back to Taiwan.*

Sometimes, I didn't understand why she didn't move back to Taiwan.

"我的女兒不是我想像的女兒." *The daughter I have is not the daughter I wished for.*

"她不聽話." *She doesn't listen.*

None of my friends' moms hit their daughters; none of my friends worry about taking care of their moms the way I do.

At the arcade though, that fifth grade summer, all this gets placed aside. Under the effulgent glow of this box, we scan the soft contours for what could come loose and fixate on the same shapes, together.

"Yeh!" she exclaims, deposits a small lion plushie in my hands.

We count two more tokens out.

We are a family that coupon clips for Top Ramen. Our clothes are from garage sales that we visit on weekends, rummaging through the discards of other peoples' lives to build our own. Professional barbers cost money, so she once accidentally gave Richard a haircut that made him look like a skunk, buzzed straight down the middle. I watch her try on shiny size five-and-a-half shoes at Saks OFF 5th, and I watch her put them down.

It feels extravagant to spend money I'm not sure we have. But Mom and I need more lion plushies.

SARAH MATSUI has been featured in NPR's *Code Switch*, *Jacobin Magazine,* and *Rethinking Schools'* magazine for "Our Picks for Books for Social Justice Teaching: Policy." Her latest writing was selected as the winner of the 2021 *Sewanee Review* Nonfiction Contest judged by Stephanie Danler and a winner of the 2022 *Fractured Lit Anthology* Contest judged by Deesha Philyaw. She is the recipient of awards and support from Tin House, Lighthouse, the San Francisco Arts Commission, Theatre Bay Area, Gotham Writers, Longleaf Writers Conference, and Kearny Street Workshop. She is currently working on her first memoir and her first novel.

13

Trauma Becomes You

KAREN MCKINNON

It is my job to gag her. Mike and some of the others have her pinned to the ground. The rest are watching us. My hand is covering her wildly moving mouth. She is trying to bite me. This enrages me. I reach my other hand into my coat pocket feeling for the bandana, wondering how the thin strip of cloth is going to muffle the screams I know will come as soon as I relax the pressure of my hand. "If you scream, we'll kill you," I say with my most menacing voice into her unblinking eyes.

I am eight or nine, not usually the lead neighborhood sociopath. I am the one who plays Barbie with the boy who stutters. I play jacks with the girl whose hand has been shriveled since birth. I don't make fun of the kid who will forever talk in a squeaky girl-voice because his doctors slipped when they were removing his tonsils.

I know the rules. We are supposed to shun Sherrie because her parents weigh over 300 pounds apiece. I, alone, have been inside their house, tempted by extravagant ice cream sundaes and ancient Elvis records my parents do not have. I have seen Sherrie's mother scream at her for leaving the screen door ajar, for crookedly parting her infrequently washed hair. I know how damaged Sherrie is and why. Yet here I am, adding injury to injury.

Sherrie has a bad habit of trying to tag along. Usually, we ditch her. But today we've had enough of her whining. Now we have her tied to the fence in Mike's backyard. She can see her house through the wood slats, see her father's car pull into the driveway, see it getting dark. She knows she will be punished for staying out this late. We want her to be grounded. We leave her there to struggle free. We go home to our warm dinners.

IT'S HALLOWEEN, AND I put on my cyclops mask and trick-or-treat with everyone until my pillowcase is black from dragging the candy haul around. I know I'm supposed to avoid Sherrie, but they live next door and I'm alone, and I know they'll have the yummiest treats, so I make one last stop. Sherrie's yard is festooned with steaming cauldrons and scratchy brooms that catch the hem of my costume robe. I tear myself loose and knock on her door. Sherrie's mom sees my mask and says,

"You never looked better," before thrusting a stuffed goody bag with a witch on it into my outstretched hand.

When I get home my mom looks me up and down and points me to the bathtub. I see myself, hideous in the mirror, and yank at my mask but it doesn't come off, and I can't get any air and I feel myself dying and wake myself up.

MY SKATES ROLL fast on the newly poured sidewalks, especially with my dog pulling me by the leash. He doesn't know to avoid Sherrie and luckily, he doesn't stop when we pass her. But then my skate catches on her foot and I don't let go, and Silky scrapes me another several yards before tiring of dragging me. I look back and the blood-tracks from my skinned knees lead straight to Sherrie's grin.

IT'S A PERFECT windy day and we are trying to fly from our umbrellas. We hunt the neighborhood for a ladder so we can try from the roof. A crowd starts to form on the side of my house. Once we're all roof-high, seeing the small boxes of our homes, our swing sets rusting in place, our parents' unfulfilled landscape dreams, I understand that I am yearning for something outside this place, outside myself, and that catastrophe would be a welcome relief. Sherrie is begging to be let up the ladder. Mike whispers, "Our guinea pig is here," then shouts, "Let her up!" He pops open the biggest umbrella we have and hands it to her. We are all looking over the edge of the roof, gauging the likelihood of a soft landing on the patch of unmown grass. Sherrie holds the umbrella and watches us watching her. I see a hint of defiance in her face about the sacrifice she's about to make and close my eyes, picturing her flying from my roof to hers and on down the line.

And then I feel the jerky push, and I am flying, and the thrill of escape lasts just long enough.

⌒

KAREN MCKINNON is the author of the novel, *Narcissus Ascending*, published in hardcover and paperback by Picador, USA, and selected by Francine Prose for the New Voice Fiction Award. She has published short stories in *Global City Review*, *On the Rocks: The KGB Bar Fiction Anthology*, and *Toho Journal*. She has taught Advanced Fiction workshops and Summer Writing Salons at the New School and has attended Bread Loaf and Sewanee Writers' Conferences as well as the Provincetown Fine Arts Work Center.

14

Luna

DAWN MILLER

From her window seat on the train, Ruth watches the cluster of teenage boys on the platform. They posture in the dusk as a tall girl, black hair swinging in a high ponytail, draws near. As she skirts the group, their boldness swells, and the boys whoop and holler.

Ruth fumbles for a caramel along the bottom of her purse, removes the silvery foil and pops it in her mouth, sucking hard to savour the sweetness as the girl fades in the distance. Once, Ruth starred in such a vignette.

A wide-shouldered fellow with a full, dark beard takes a seat across the aisle, facing her. He looks so like Thomas when they met a lifetime ago. Broad, powerful hands. Square-shaped nails. She concentrates on the view out the window, but his presence tugs on her, dragging her eyes back. She can almost feel the warmth of his palms against her face. The sharp, muskiness of sweat, moist lips kissing carpentry callouses.

Thomas.

Gone for two years. Each day longer than the one before. She'd prayed she'd go first.

The bearded man's eyes skim across her face—a glance, less than a whisper. Once his gaze would have lingered over her creamy skin and thick auburn hair tied back with a red velvet ribbon. Once he would have sought her gaze and smiled.

She crunches the last of the candy, sticky bits clinging between her dentures as the train shudders and lumbers forward. The man flashes a sharp look at her and shifts to stare out the window, arms crossed. Heat blooms up Ruth's chest into her cheeks. He must think her a crazy old bat, gawking like that. She licks her sugary lips, dampening tender cracks resistant to beeswax and aloe, and focuses on the rushing trees and how the moonlight casts ghostly shadows across the landscape.

Thomas called her Luna—beautiful and mysterious as the moon. And now *he* is the moon, drifting through the heavens, while she is left, pinned to earth like a beetle squirming under glass.

Her children will be shocked at first. Horrified. The room they arranged at the nursing home looked nice enough on the tour. But it is tiny, and she has a lifetime of possessions. Sheila, her oldest, separated her belongings into categories: Give Away, Donate, Take-to-the-Dump, Keep—the size of the piles in ascending order. Like a set of Russian dolls, her world is shrinking.

"Mom told *me* I'd get the Hummels," Sheila informed her younger brother, Charles, the last time they came. Poor Charles threw his hands up in the air, giving in as always, a born peacekeeper. Like his father.

Ruth witnessed the exchange from her easy chair. They thought she was engrossed in the fighting on *Judge Judy*, but she knew what was going on right under her nose. For a moment, she considered snatching the row of porcelain figurines from the display case and smashing them on the linoleum. Snapping the head off "Goose Girl," making "Apple Tree Boy" plunge from the branches. Thomas bought the Hummels for her, each figure tied to a memory between them. They meant nothing to Sheila. Other than money.

After they left, Ruth took a permanent marker and wrote *Sheila* or *Charles* in shaky letters on the bottom of each figurine. Fifty-fifty. Otherwise, Sheila might scoop them all up.

Such a bitter thing to love your child but not like her very much.

At the next stop, the bearded man disembarks. He stands on the platform, searching right and left. *Go where your heart is*, Ruth wants to shout. That's what she's doing. Writing the final act herself.

The train picks up speed and her heart leaps at the thought of seeing Thomas. She leans forward, willing the train to go faster. The full moon made her decision. Tonight is the perfect night.

Clutching her purse, she readies for the next stop—a sleepy town on the edge of the Saugeen River. Thomas caught many a trout in those waters swirling with hidden life. Many years ago, they attempted to swim there, but the current almost carried her away, and he'd wrapped his muscled arms around her, pulling her close.

She laces her palsied fingers together, bones fragile as a bird's neck, and inspects the crescent moons at the base of each fingernail. Lunula. She whispers the word, her tongue kissing her palate with each syllable, the word ripe as a berry in her mouth.

She is water, bending to the pull of the moon. To the mystery ahead. To Thomas.

She will become Luna again.

DAWN MILLER holds a BA in English from Queen's University in Canada and is a 2021 Pushcart Prize nominee. She is a member of the Canadian Authors Association, Canada Council for the Arts, and Women's Fiction Writers Association. Her short fiction has appeared or is forthcoming in *Typehouse Literary Magazine, The Main Review, Verandah Literary and Art Journal, Loud Coffee Press Literary Magazine,* the Canadian Authors Association's *Fifteen Stories High Short Story Anthology 2021,* and *Blank Spaces Short Story Anthology 2022.* Currently, she is querying her debut novel.

15

July 1964

CARA OLEXA

In a blur, a blind of grass, the horse. Dunes. At your right, ocean collapsing on the edge of Virginia. The fleabitten mare ahead, returning with her empty saddle. Here comes a horse: head bobbing, *miff* of sand from lifting hooves, to pause two strides off. The mare, watchful from a red-flecked cheek, and past her, up the beach, you see their horses stop and turn, Aunt Kate and Aunt Kate's friend with Mikey on the lead behind her. A horse throws, threw, a girl, and she (you, the girl) lands in sand, *thumff* on her ass on the dune, tumbling. The mare looks at you, on your ass but upright. A girl is thrown but fine. Rolls, sits up, is fine. Miracles happen, every day. Did you think all those bedtime prayers were for naught? Bouncing off your bedroom ceiling? Here, now, on the beach, *this* is a miracle: three days and five hundred miles ago, you hid in the attic with pencils and waxed paper and traced from your horse book, appaloosas and thoroughbreds and palominos, sweating on dusty knees while the domestic tumult continued below, first floor, second, first, crashes and curses until the sun set in the attic window and you were thirsty and had to pee. Did you never think your prayers would be answered? Your selfish, jealous prayers—tell the truth, did you ever pray for Mom or Dad or the baby, or for Mikey who's only six? Tell the truth, you asked God for horses (but did you deserve them? Tell the truth, tell God you left Mikey downstairs while you hid in the attic, every time). That night an ambulance took Mom to visit Gramma again, and when Mikey whispered *Is Mom a drunk?* you told him to shut up. *You don't even know what a drunk is, stupid.* But this time God said *Yes* and lifted you from Pittsburgh by the scruff of your neck. Dad woke you at dawn with a suitcase. *Get your clothes on, Meredith.* The end of Mom, not known but felt. Dad, dark against your brightening bedroom window, and Aunt Kate smoking in the doorway, ashing into a coffee mug because the ashtrays were broken. *Shoes on, Mer, chop chop* she said. *Big adventure today.* Is this what you wanted? You and Mikey climbed into Aunt Kate's wondrous white Cadillac, but *No, your dad's not coming* and *No, the baby's too little*—but *Don't worry about the baby, Mer, she's at your gramma's* (which makes sense, doesn't it, because isn't Mom at Gramma's?). Yes, you prayed, good girl, but did you ever really believe? Now that God has picked you up and dropped you onto the haysilk back of a horse, maybe you will. In the dunes the fleabitten mare is watchful but you're small, sprawled, so she squares her nose to you to observe the surf. Did you believe in the ocean before you saw it? You *knew* about the ocean, from school, movies, television, but did you *believe*? Miracles defy explanation: why doesn't the ocean run out of waves? Where do they come from? Down on the sand you see one wave, maybe half a dozen, but behind a wave comes a million million more, like this one. This one. This one. The mare lips dune grass. She threw you: you know it, but it happened so quick you don't believe it yet. You're not crying yet. Aunt Kate's friend points at you; you keep forgetting her name, but it's her bed-and-breakfast, her fleabitten mare. *Fleabitten doesn't mean fleas,* she said when you insisted this horse is ugly. You wanted the chestnut, but Mikey got the chestnut, so she (the friend) told you that she (the horse) was famous once, won a race, but you were sure she was making it up. Now Aunt Kate turns her bay gelding, trots down the beach toward you. You're fine but a moment from now, when she says, *Mer, are you all right?* and you try to tell her, you'll start crying, tears all over your sandy face (red and ugly as your horse's). But that hasn't happened, yet. Right now it's still Now: here, now, you look up at what you wanted. A gauze-gray horse in a gauze sky. Ocean folding on a slim blade of shoreline. A horse walks toward you. Miracle: you believe. A horse walks toward you because you believe.

CARA OLEXA earned her MFA from New Mexico State University. Her fiction has been published in *Ploughshares* and received honorable mention from *Glimmer Train* and *Gulf Coast.* She's lived in Oregon, New Mexico, Illinois, and Tennessee, but will always be from Ohio.

16

Dust

TERRI PEASE

There was a lot of dust on them mens. Me, keepin' off the wooden sidewalk while keeping an eye, *a close eye, mind,* on them rowdy boys of Mist' Showet, all I could see was dusty mens. They wasn't wearin' more than rags over they parts, and some not even that. In my head I was studying—to see could I get a half-spoiled bit of sugar to bring back to my pallet. Could maybe the fella what totes barrel for Boss Kerman in the store see some what had-a fell on the floor and sweep it up for "out back." Could maybe put some in a little in a sack I could hide in my dress front. So I was thinkin' about could I make a little sugar tit for my twins I couldn't feed when he spat right in front of me, so's I could see he was there.

The coffle was stopped in the road, driver muttering with the dark ugly over one man on his knees on that road. He swinging his whip on that man, the blood running over his back making streaks in the dust from the quarry where he worked them.

And the spit, landing at my feet is all made me look.

And then I had to stop. I dropped to the dirt, not looking for more than a breath's time, then reaching for my behind, to worry and scratch like I had some kind of flea on me. I knew it was him, sent to the quarry so he and I would never so much as breathe air in the same place. All cause Master Showet wanted what he wanted.

Mama told me 'fore I could smell myself good, *don't let no white folks see what you love.*

But I thought the wind in the trees stopped when Basie ran by that day. I'd been seeing him round the place my whole life, and he was just one more rusty-behind boy driving hogs and fetchin' for the stable man. But that day when he came racing round that corner and shouting *hog runnin' move the chirrens,* I took two babies by the arms and pushed them into the door of the nearest cabin, then looked and felt myself. Under my arms started to prickle and my hands went up there. I watched his legs flash by, saw how he fell on that old hog and threw rope round one leg and its neck, so's it had to follow where he took it or stop its own breath.

And after, anytime, just seeing how Basie could shout those animals to do anything he wanted, made my hands fly up under my arms, made me wish I was a little cow too, or a hog so he could fall on me. And surely Mama called me heifer then. But I was seeing nothin' and no one but Basie.

I sat in that street. Just scratching like I had nothin' but fleas, so's I could worry my dress up to my knees, let him see me, see I knew him, remember how on that one Sunday, sittin' on the cabin stoop and spittin' watermelon seeds, I was laughin' cause I was winnin', and his fingers got near to my knees, then driver come up with some other hands. *Good thing,* he say, *Master done told me keep my eyes on you, gal.*

Boy. Now he talking to Basie and got him pulled up, Basie shirt twisted round his neck, he almost on tippy toes, *Boy, I know that stable need you, but we done just found out Boss Nolmann there need you down his quarry more.*

And like that Basie was gone.

Basie's Mama never so much as look at me again, 'cause all the hands knew Master had to sell that big strong boy was gon' be a main-hand cause him and me was gettin' too friendly. And Master had me to the back field, to the curehouse that night, and load of nights after, and I had them babies done got sold soon as they weaned, a boy, another boy, and one I didn't know what it was they took it from me so fast to feed on another place, or maybe just drowned it if it look too white. And I makes all my milk now for the babies in the big house.

But I got mine back. I sat in that street just like a heifer and worried that flea ain't really a flea and drug my dress up so Basie could see I knew he was in that quarry coffle, and that I knew how he had been smiling and spittin' seeds, and they hadn't killed him yet. And that he knew I loved him.

TERRI PEASE holds a Ph.D. in Human Development from Cornell University, is a former college professor and retired national consultant on child development, domestic violence, and trauma, including historical trauma.

17

Spatchcock

SARAH ROSENTHAL

The whole bird lay naked on the cutting board. Iris had received the wooden board as a wedding present. It held the scars of years and years of tiny careful cuts.

The body hardly looked like a recognizable creature without the head, the feathers, the feet. She could almost forget it had been alive. Iris traced her left index finger over the creature's skin, a puckered goosebump film over too-pink flesh. She then worked her finger over the pathetic folded wings, the stiff legs pointed towards her. The leg joints had already been severed from the body with a pair of kitchen shears. With one smooth motion, she flipped the carcass so it lay prone, belly up. Iris held the sturdy kitchen knife in her right hand and considered the spine. It was her first Sunday alone, and she was hungry.

Her husband had been difficult to please. He had been a vegetarian. While Iris spent years as a housewife mastering meatless dishes for him, he had been satisfying his appetites with his coworker, the one with creamy skin and cherry lipstick that left bloody grenadine smears on Iris's sateen pillowcases.

Iris ran her fingers up and down the bird's backbone. She was good with a knife. Carefully, she dragged the blade down one side of the bone, and then the other. The tip of the knife worked through the fat lines with ease, and how quickly the bones gave way to the steel blade with some light sawing motions. *Sss, sss, crunch.* With each hack at the animal's ribs, it became easier for Iris to breathe.

She flipped the body again so it lay on its stomach, the carcass looser, easier to control. Iris pressed down on the spine with her left hand and both legs with her right arm, pushing all her weight so she crushed the animal and it lay perfectly flat, making it easier to roast evenly. The body obliged with a satisfying *crunch* of rearranged bone. She smiled at her work and took the herb butter she'd prepped earlier to rub beneath the skin. That morning she'd grabbed rosemary, thyme, and parsley when she was working out in her garden, and now they perfumed her filthy hands as she caressed it into the muscles, bones, and fat. Once the butter was spread, she washed her hands yet again, and noted she really ought to clean out the kitchen sink better: it was still covered with dirt from earlier. Time to cook the bird now. It entered the oven at a blasting 400 degrees.

There was dirt beneath her nails still. She'd done so much digging that morning, and she was so, so hungry. Iris looked out the window at all that freshly turned soil, shook her head at the mess she'd made. They redid the garden a few years back, all *his* idea of what it should look like even though she was the one who spent all her time out there growing something out of nothing. Now that she'd destroyed his creation, perhaps it was time for a change. She'd have to replant her rosemary bush, the dill plant, even the roses. There was so much to clean still, in the bedroom and in the garden. But once the meat really got to cooking, once the fat melted off the bones and redistributed itself, once she properly washed her hands and her knife, once she burned the bloody bedsheets twisted open like lips parted, this house would smell like a home again.

SARAH ROSENTHAL is a writer and educator whose work has been featured in *Bitch Magazine, The Sun, GEN Mag, Creative Nonfiction, Gay Mag, LitHub, Electric Lit, McSweeney's Internet Tendency, CrimeReads, Columbia Journal,* and beyond. She earned her MFA in nonfiction writing from Columbia University School of the Arts and her BA in written arts from Bard College. She lives in Brooklyn.

18

Your Lover, The Clown

IONA RULE

You meet him at your niece's birthday party, where the kids run
feral, coked-up on pink juice and icing. While he performs his
act, your sister is with her mum friends, drinking warm wine in
the kitchen and whispering loudly about *that* mother in the PTA.
The men are outside, comparing their latest acquisitions: BBQs,
lawnmowers, mistresses.

He makes balloon animals, a menagerie passing through his hands. You watch the deft way his fingers move, creating knots and curls, producing life from nothing. The children request eagles, frogs and unicorns, which he produces with an effortless flourish. He asks you what animal you would like. You look into his whitewashed face with its scarlet smile and diamond eyes and reply, "A hedgehog," because you've never been easy and spending time with your family makes you bitter. He keeps smiling and creates a dolphin, presenting it with a comical bow. It's not even close.

"I will practise," he says, which may be the kindest thing anyone will say to you today. You want to tell him that a group of hedgehogs is called an array, but that you have never seen a group. You have only ever seen one.

YOU TAKE HIM to a bar after and ask if he'd like to take off the face paint and the oversized rainbow dungarees. He says he's comfortable as he is, and you're relieved. You order a Negroni, and the ice cubes click against your teeth with each sip. He tells you about his family. You expected fire-eaters and acrobats and are disappointed when he talks of a plumber and a librarian. You tell him about your parents, how you always wanted to be different but never quite managed.

THAT NIGHT YOU take him home. You undo his bow tie and remove his blue bowler hat, but ask him to leave his face paint on. As you have sex you stare into his face which is always smiling and wonder if it could always be like this. In the morning, after he leaves, you apply your lipstick, moving the crimson paste beyond your lip line, curling up the edges in a permanent grin.

YOU MEET YOUR lover, the clown, every Thursday. He smells of greasepaint and candyfloss. He always comes in costume, straight from a shopping centre opening or a circus audition. Every time, you ask him to leave it on. It amuses you to think that you may be passing your lover on the street or the bus, and never know it. That you have never seen his real face.

THE LAST TIME he comes over you tell him you're ready and ask him to take off the mask. But he won't.

"You never take off yours," he says.

He kisses you, smearing paint on your face, below your eye, like a tear, ties his red shoes and leaves.

You find the gift he has left on the bedside table. A balloon animal. The hedgehog he promised, and beside it, a pin. Because he knew you so well, after all.

IONA RULE lives and writes in the Scottish Highlands. She has been shortlisted in *Retreat West, Fractured Lit,* and *TSS Publishing.* She has been published here and there, including in *The Phare, Epoch Press, Ellipses,* and *perhappened.*

19

No Matter How Pretty They Look

KRISTINA T. SACCONE

It was our first once-a-month grandmother-granddaughter date at the JCC. I hopped on the treadmill while you did Jazzercise, all ladies over the age of 60—or maybe 70, but at the time, I couldn't tell the difference—and one man, Norman. Ink blots on his bare head, pants up to his ears. The ladies laughed in the locker room about his little grunt each time he leaned on his right foot. They said it sounded like their husbands trying to come. You sat there with them, all of you naked from the waist-up, folds of silly putty skin rolling over a couple ragged surgery scars, some galaxy-size stretch marks, and one larger-than-a-tarantula wine-colored mole above a pale, lumpy buttock. You talked like old friends—though you said you barely knew any of them—breasts resting on their stomachs, thighs, towels wrapped around their waists, giggling about Norman and as though at an afternoon klatsch, fully dressed neck to ankle.

I watched this with my robe tied shut, in wet shower shoes, shielding myself with the locker door, mortified by all that skin and laughing and wetness and unadulterated fat. At the time, I was worried about the guy I was dating, his obsession with an ex, whether he fucked me for fun or to forget her. When you mentioned my "mysterious man" to the ladies, they turned their fleshy bodies at me and poked for details. I showed them Trey's Match.com photo, and their crooked fingers reached for more detail. They cooed over it, but you, you never minced words. You said, "No matter how pretty they look now, they all turn into Norman one day."

I stepped behind the shower curtain and let the robe slide off, water rolling off my belly. Trey's ex—or so he said—had a flat tummy and round butt, but mine was curvy, channeling suds from the crease between my breasts to my belly button until the soap disappeared. I got out of the shower with nothing but a towel on my head. Until then, I had never been naked in front of anyone but boyfriends or the doctor—no, not even in front of Mom, not since I grew breasts—but you and your friends didn't blink because I was just one of the ladies.

Norman winked at us on our way out the door. I left a voicemail for Trey in the parking lot, not sure I wanted him to call back, before we picked up pastries and ate them in the car, buttery flakes crumbling all over our laps. It was the best date I ever had.

⌒⌒

KRISTINA T. SACCONE is a writer of flash fiction and nonfiction. She also curates *Flash Roundup*, a weekly email featuring the latest releases in flash fiction, and she's querying a flash anthology of stories about caring for our aging parents. Her work appears or is forthcoming in *Fractured Lit, Cease, Cows, Gone Lawn, Six Sentences, LEON Literary Review, Red Fez, The Bangor Literary Journal,* and *Emerge Literary Journal.* Find her on Twitter at @kristinasaccone and @flashroundup.

20

Coefficient

PHILLIP STERLING

The foam pillow, one of several retrieved from his parents' house after the sale, smelled of Bengay. Meant for the guest bedroom, which his wife at the time redecorated in what she called "Victorian Chic"—an effort, under compromise, to both appropriate and purge the room of gothic memorabilia abandoned (*at last!*) by the youngest son of his first marriage—the pillow had been remaindered to the upper shelf of the closet, beside the Comedy mask he'd been unable to part with (its mate, Tragedy, featured in the property settlement of the first divorce). When he slept with his head on the foam pillow, he dreamt of leaning back onto the vinyl seats of Mike's '65 Pontiac Bonneville and drag racing along Grand View Parkway in Traverse City, Michigan, and of how Mike would remove the ring-buoy-sized air filter from the carburetor, convinced that it would help them go faster.

The feather pillow, one of two *100% Real Down* pillows his second wife left behind, smelled of windowsills—moth dust and insect casings. It languished feebly on "her" side of the queen-sized maple cannonball bed they'd purchased to replace what she'd called "the bridal suite," a double-sized frame (no headboard) that she'd asked him to donate to the Salvation Army. ("A way to reduce," she said, "your thinking of anyone else when we screw.") When he slept on the feather pillow, he dreamt that he was stranded and panicky in an airport in Europe—Brussels, maybe—because he couldn't locate his nine suitcases, his four kids, his wife, or the bread he'd bought to go with the hard sausage and cheese they'd meant to smuggle back into the States and which was packed already in one of the suitcases the older kids had been instructed to supervise carefully, as packages left unattended would be scooped into what looked to be an industrial floor cleaner modified by a U.N. demolition team, taken out onto the tarmac, and exploded into inedible fragments of *porc* and Edam.

The other feather pillow (the "match") anchored the couch in the family room. It smelled a little like the beer he'd spilled when he'd fallen asleep watching a Julia Roberts film—either from the VHS collection his first wife left behind or from the DVD collection his second wife added to—and a little like the fishy breath of the kitten he'd rescued from the county animal shelter (and named "Julia" and raised for nearly a year before its disappearance...). He doesn't dream, when he falls asleep on that pillow. Or at least he doesn't recall any dreams.

Now it's summer again. And most nights he can be found in a sleeping bag in the yard, his pillow a rolled up beach towel. The towel smells faintly of dune grass and coconut oil, though due to more pronounced odors of the neighborhood's automobile exhaust and recently mown grass, it would be difficult for anyone besides him to smell it. He's had the towel since college, off-white with a (faded) cartoonish figure of a pink cow laying in the sun, its udders exposed. Below the cow are the words: "Roast Beef." For years he thought it was funny. When he sleeps with the towel beneath his head, he dreams of his first wife before she was his wife and of how warm her skin had seemed, how lightly damp, the first time she let him—*led* him—to touch her *here*, as if the stars would always be aligned just so, as if the source of the light that reached him was not already gone.

PHILLIP STERLING'S books include two collections of short fiction, *In Which Brief Stories Are Told* (Wayne State University Press 2011) and *Amateur Husbandry* (Mayapple 2019), two full-length collections of poetry (*And Then Snow, Mutual Shores*), and five chapbook-length series of poems, the most recent of which, *Short on Days*, was released from Main Street Rag in June 2020, after several months of quarantine.

21

Remember Your Goals

MICHELE ZIMMERMAN

Write down your goals for tomorrow. Write down your goals on a small pocket-sized notepad so that you can take it with you. Don't make these goals for tomorrow a "to-do" list. Don't do this because some of the things you're bound to include in your goals (like "shower") are never included in other people's "to-do" lists. "Goals" because that feels softer, more forgiving. Write down your goals, and then place the pocket-sized notepad down on your bedside table.

When you wake up in the morning, reach over, pick it up, and let it be the first thing you see. Pick up your novel, leaf through a couple pages while you sip coffee. Savor the few moments you have before the day starts, before you have to start meeting your goals.

Welcome the cat onto your lap, pet the cat underneath the chin. Pet the cat on the top of the head. Do not, under any circumstances, pet the cat on the ears.

Get up and wash your hand with clear, liquid soap when the cat scratches your palm after you have definitely pet her on the ears. Remember to buy more clear liquid soap when it struggles to come out of the nozzle. Write "remember to buy clear liquid soap" on your list of goals.

Do not think about the person you saw at the train station yesterday. Do not write out a message to the person you saw at the train station yesterday. Do not, under any circumstances, send the message. Do not wonder what her life is like, now. Do not wonder who knows her better than you do, now. Do not let your thoughts stray from your goals. Write down all of these "do-nots" into your list of goals. Put down your pen now. Put it down. Do not write out these things. Forget the questions you have like,

Did you see me across the landing at the train station?

Is that why you left?

Or, did you realize that you were on the wrong platform and suddenly leave to correct the mistake?

Was it too windy for you, over there?

Did your unruly hair catch in the breeze and cover your eyes, so that your reading was interrupted?

What were you reading?

If you saw me, what did I look like to you from across the landing at the train station?

Did you notice me from my walk, or from the way I stand?

Could you see the new tattoos? Even the ones underneath my clothes?

What would you have done if I had waved?

What would you have done if I had come up to you and asked what you were reading?

What would you have done if I hadn't pretended to not see you?

Would you write about me again?

Are you doing that right now?

Stop that now. Stop wondering these things. These things are not part of, or related to, your goals. Do you know what happens when you abandon the goals? If you abandon the goals list, you spiral. If you spiral, you forget to do important things for work. If you forget to do things for work, your bosses will take notice. If the bosses take notice, they'll be nice about it at first, and ask if you're doing okay. If you say you're okay, they might believe you. If you say you're okay, they will probably believe you, but they will still keep an eye out for mistakes. If you make mistakes, or forget things, like which shifts you're supposed to turn up for, they will become stern. They might have conversations with you about responsibility, and trust, and pay rates.

If you don't get paid $16 per hour, you can't pay rent. If you don't get $16 per hour, you can't eat. If you don't get paid, you can't feed the cat that you shouldn't ever pet on the ears. If you don't get paid, you will have to ask your older brother for help, and his wife will roll her eyes so hard, you will practically be able to see it through the telephone. If you ask him if she is rolling her eyes, it will start a thing between the two of them, and then he will call you back in a few days' time and tell you he can't help you. When he says he can't do anything for you with an apologetic tone, he will lightly suggest that you ask your parents, and you will recoil and feel like a failure. When he calls he will speak in low tones, even if his wife is not around, and ask you if you're doing okay. If you say you're fine, he won't believe you. He will wait patiently, quietly, on the line until you start to really tell him the truth. He will ask you, what happened? Did you see her again? Weren't those goals that your therapist started you on working out well for you?

Throw out those questions you weren't supposed to write down. Rip that piece of paper out of the pocket-sized notebook and crumple it into a small ball. Throw it into the trashcan. If you miss the trashcan, the cat will think of the ball of paper as a new plaything. The cat will swat the crumpled questions back and forth between her claws, and eventually the piece of paper will be shredded up into many tiny pieces. Don't let the cat eat the shreds of paper; she will try. Don't dwell on what having seen that person at the train station could have been. Don't think there was a chance of further interaction with her going well for you. Finish the coffee that's probably cold now. Rinse the mug. Get into the shower. Complete your goals for today. Then, write down your list of goals for the next day. Place it on your beside table, so when you wake up, it can be the first thing you see.

MICHELE ZIMMERMAN is a Queer writer and holds an MFA in fiction from Sarah Lawrence College. Her work appears in *Superfroot, Post Road, Catapult's Tiny Nightmares: Very Short Tales of Horror*, and others. She is the winner of the *Blood Orange Review* 2021 Literary Contest. In the past she has been a Sundress Publications Best of the Net nominee and a two-time finalist for the *Glimmer Train* Short Story Award for New Writers. Find her on Twitter @m_l_zimmerman.

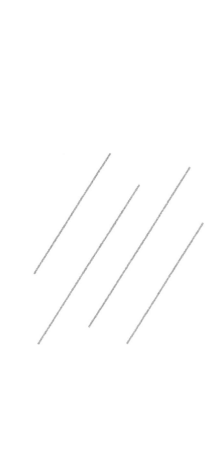

Milton Keynes UK
Ingram Content Group UK Ltd.
UKHW051147300923
429627UK00023B/989